For Lillyanna—YP

For Phoebe, Vivian and Zeva. I hope you
enjoy this reading challenge.—DM

Scholastic Australia
An imprint of Scholastic Australia Pty Limited
PO Box 579 Gosford NSW 2250
ABN 11 000 614 577
www.scholastic.com.au

Part of the Scholastic Group
Sydney · Auckland · New York · Toronto · London · Mexico City
New Delhi · Hong Kong · Buenos Aires · Puerto Rico

Published by Scholastic Australia in 2022.
Text and illustrations copyright © Scholastic Australia, 2022.
Text by Yvette Poshoglian.
Cover design, illustrations and inside illustrations by Danielle McDonald.

The moral rights of Yvette Poshoglian have been asserted.
The moral rights of Danielle McDonald have been asserted.

 A catalogue record for this
book is available from the
National Library of Australia

ISBN: 978-1-76112-311-5

Typeset in Buccardi.

Printed by McPherson's Printing Group, Maryborough, VIC.

Scholastic Australia's policy, in association with McPherson's Printing Group, is to use
papers that are renewable and made efficiently with wood from responsibly managed
sources, so as to minimise its environmental footprint.

22 23 24 25 26 / 2

By
Yvette Poshoglian

Illustrated by
Danielle McDonald

A Scholastic Australia Book

Chapter One

Ella and Olivia are sisters. Ella is seven and her little sister Olivia is five-and-a-half. They love **BOOKS!**

Ella reads chapter books now. Olivia is trying junior chapter books. Max can't read yet, but he **LOVES** to turn the pages by himself.

Ella and her best friend Zoe are **HOOKED** on a series called *Dog Detectives*. They can't get enough of the canine sleuths! Olivia likes books about fairies and adventures.

Both sisters love to spend time in the library at school, choosing new books to take home.

The school librarian is Ms Minassian. Ms Minassian **ADORES** books. Ella and Olivia adore Ms Minassian! She loves to decorate the library with pictures of characters from everyone's **FAVOURITE** stories.

On library day, Olivia sees a big, bold **NEW** sign on the library door.

JOIN THE
SCHOOL READING CHALLENGE

How many books can you read in one month?
The class that reads the most books in each year group will win a prize!

Entries close on the last day of the month.

You can read a:

Picture book   Chapter book   Young Adult novel

About:

Nonfiction   Mystery   Historical
Fiction   Adventure   Comedy
Middle Fiction   Science Fiction   Action

'I hope you and Ella
are going to **JOIN** the
Reading Challenge,' says
Ms Minassian from behind
the library counter.

Olivia takes two flyers with
all the information
about the
Challenge—
one for her
and one
for Ella.

Olivia looks at the list again. There are lots of **TYPES** of stories that she doesn't know much about. And some of the books might be too old for her to read.

'You have to read two books from each category,' says the librarian. 'And the classes who read the most in each year group will win a prize!'

Olivia looks around the library. All the books she could possibly need are in here. There are bookcases **BULGING** with books. There are shelves **SHIMMERING** with stories.

Olivia and her classmates gather as **MANY** books as they can borrow from the library. Meanwhile, Ms Minassian fills library bags and signs students up to the Reading Challenge.

Olivia puts her name down
next to her class group:

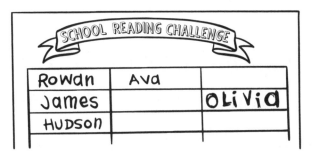

SCHOOL READING CHALLENGE		
Rowan	Ava	
James		Olivia
Hudson		

Then she signs up Ella, too.

SCHOOL READING CHALLENGE		
Libby	Scarlet	Ella
Hannah	Clancy	

There's just one problem.
Olivia has **NEVER** read a
junior chapter book all by
herself.

Chapter Two

'Ella! Guess what?' Olivia is so excited to show her big sister the School Reading Challenge flyer.

Together, the sisters start to gather their books. Ella brings out her **HUGE** pile of *Dog Detective* books that she and Zoe have collected. Olivia piles her huge library reading stack on the dining table. Max brings over his favourite board books. They have been slightly CHEWED around the edges.

'YUCK, Max!' says Olivia. But she builds Max a special little pile, too.

Together, they sort books into different piles. Then they will choose books from each other's piles.

Olivia looks sadly at her stack. If only she could read longer books! She has read all of her favourite picture books. She is just starting to try her first chapter books, but they take a **LONG TIME** to read.

She gives Max a pile of her picture books.

'Let's set up a Reading Challenge library!' says Ella.

Together, the sisters make some space on the lounge room bookshelf. Then they stack all the cushions on the lounge next to it to make a **COMFY, COSY** place to read.

Next, they pile all the new books they have borrowed from the library and place them on the shelves, along with all the books from their own bedrooms.

'I think we need more, Olivia!' says Ella.

'**MORE?**' Olivia asks.

Ella and Olivia turn to Mum and Dad's bookshelves. Olivia takes all of Dad's books on plants (they have lots of pictures). Ella takes all of Mum's sports books.

'That's a good start,' says Ella, looking at the TOWERS of books in front of her, Olivia and Max.

'It's time to get COMFY,' says Olivia, burrowing into the couch. Ella and Olivia have a lot of reading ahead.

That's when the trouble begins!

Chapter Three

Ella and Olivia are **GLUED** to their books. Ella **STARTS** with a chapter book steeped in magic. Soon, she is swept up in a world of wizardry and wonder.

Olivia **BEGINS** by choosing a picture book from the library. Soon, she

is carried away to a world of
baby farm animals that also
have SUPERPOWERS!

Every time they finish a
book, the girls add the title
to their Reading Challenge
list. Each book adds to their
total. Ella finishes her first
book before Olivia.

SCHOOL READING CHALLENGE

Name: Ella   Class: 2 crimson

Title of book	Genre	Type of book	✓
WIZARDRY WONDERS	fiction	chapter Book	✓

The house is quiet. It's **TOO QUIET**. It starts to drive Mum and Dad crazy!

'Ella and Olivia!' Mum calls. 'Time to do your jobs! Have you unpacked your school bags yet?'

But Ella and Olivia don't hear Mum. Ella's head is buried so far in her book, she doesn't see the big piles of dirty clothes on her floor.

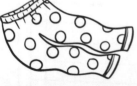

'Ella, it's time to set the table!' says Dad.

'Olivia, it's time to feed Bob!' says Mum.

But there is no answer. Both girls can't take their EYES off their books. So Dad sets the table and Mum feeds Bob.

Ella and Olivia barely notice their dinner. They don't help clear the table or DRY the dishes.

'That's it!' says Mum.
'I'm **HAPPY** to see you
reading, but you still have
jobs and homework to do.'

'We'll do our jobs tomorrow, Mum,' says Ella. Then she puts her **NOSE** back in the book.

Olivia is onto her second picture book that night. She takes her time with sounding out all the words and looking at the pictures on each page.

But Olivia knows that she
has to be **FASTER** if she
wants her class to win.
She takes a stack of books
from her pile on the shelf
and puts them by her bed.
Maybe she can stay up late
reading with her torch.

'Goodnight, Ella!' Olivia
calls from across the
hallway.
'Goodnight, Olivia,' says
Ella. 'Happy reading!'

The next day at school, everyone checks the SCOREBOARD on the library door. Each class adds its book count to the official tally. There's also a bright new sticker on the sign.

Have you tried AUDIOBOOKS? Listen to a BOOK on a walk.

Ella borrows lots of nonfiction books—books about netball, China and ancient Egypt.

Olivia borrows lots of junior chapter books. She SCOOPS up the *Cooking Queen* series and *Wondrous Mermaids* collection. But Ella has an idea. She borrows some audiobooks.

That afternoon, Mum and Dad are **AMAZED!** The girls have done all their chores.

'I thought you were too busy reading,' says Mum.

'We are reading,' says Olivia.

'We are listening to **AUDIOBOOKS** while we do our chores!' says Ella proudly.

As Olivia tidies, she notices Ella's book pile is getting lower much faster than hers. How will she keep up?

Chapter Four

Ella already has a **HUGE** list of books that she has read for the Reading Challenge.

'Show me your list, Olivia!' she says.

Olivia doesn't want to show Ella how small her list is. She isn't getting very far in the Reading Challenge at all.

But Ella **INSISTS**.

'My class is **NEVER** going to finish top of the School Reading Challenge,' says Olivia. 'I haven't read enough books!' She doesn't want her teacher or Ms Minassian to be disappointed in her.

'Don't be silly, Olivia,' says Ella. 'I have the perfect idea!'

That afternoon, both girls and Max decide to **NESTLE** into their reading space. All of Olivia's new books are just waiting to be read.

But this time, Ella reaches over to Olivia's pile and starts to read **OUT LOUD**.

Max watches as Ella turns the front cover and starts to read the first story in the *Cooking Queen* series.

Ella reads the first page out loud. 'Now it's your turn, Olivia,' she says.
Olivia is a bit surprised!

She carefully reads the words out loud. Ella sometimes helps her **SOUND OUT** the words.

Soon, they are onto the next chapter. Suddenly, Olivia doesn't feel so bad! In fact, she has forgotten all about WORRYING about reading. Both girls and Max turn page after page after page.

By dinnertime, they are halfway through the first book and no-one wants to put the book down.

Ella and Olivia read every chance they get. Mum and Dad love that they are helping each other.

As the days go on, Ella and Olivia keep reading. They **ZOOM** through books. They love reading together.

And they keep up with their chores by listening to audiobooks while they **TIDY** their rooms.

Ella discovers that she loves **NONFICTION** books, especially about animals. She's hooked on reading books about African animals. She learned something about the Big Five: lions, leopards, rhinoceros, elephants and buffalo.

Olivia can't get enough of the junior chapter books. Every night, she and Ella read one together. They have read all eight books in the *Cooking Queen* series! They are now Olivia's favourite books.

Every night before the
sisters turn out their lights,
they look at their lists.

They are definitely getting
longer and longer—but
have they read enough to
WIN?

Chapter Five

At the end of the month, it is the last day of the Reading Challenge!

The girls return **ALL** their library books.

Ms Minassian has been run off her feet. Every single student has borrowed PILES of books. The returns chute is almost full!

The tally has been taken down from the library door.

Ella and Olivia peer through. They can see Ms Minassian with the principal, Mr White. The girls are sure they are talking about the winners of the Reading Challenge.

READING CHALLENGE

'Good luck, Ella!' says Olivia. 'Thanks for helping me with my reading!' Olivia is a bit sad that the Reading Challenge will be over soon.

'I think you've read more books than anyone else in Kinder Green!' says Ella. 'Together, we make a mighty reading team!'

They have read **LOADS** of books, fallen into **LOTS** of stories and **LEARNED** many new things. And they've done it all together.

But it's not over yet . . .

Olivia's class are given **FREE TIME** by the teacher. This means they are allowed to do any activity they choose.

Olivia has an idea! She gathers her friends in her class around her. 'There's still time to add a few more books to the Reading Challenge tally,' she says.

'Everybody, grab a book!'

'Well done, Olivia,' says her teacher. She is really proud of Olivia sharing in the reading joy with her class.

Soon it's time for the special Reading Challenge assembly. Everyone is very **NERVOUS**, especially Ella and Olivia!

Ella hopes her class, 2 Crimson, has won the challenge. Olivia crosses her fingers that her class, Kinder Green has won.

Ms Minassian steps up to the microphone to make the announcements.

'The highest number of books read by a class is . . .'
She opens the envelope.
'Class 2 Crimson!'

Ella and her classmates go WILD!

'You have won a
SPECIAL trip to a new
library in the city!' says Ms
Minassian.

Olivia feels **SAD**. She is happy for Ella. But she is sad that her class did not win. She had worked so hard on her reading.

Ms Minassian calls for everyone to be **QUIET**. She still has one certificate in her hand.

'I have one PRIZE left to announce. The teachers and I have had a talk, and we decided to give a certificate to the Most Improved Reader. This reader tried new books and encouraged others to do the same.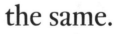

She never gave up.'

That's when Olivia hears her name! Olivia walks up on stage. Ella CHEERS for her sister.

'Congratulations, Olivia!' says Ms Minassian. She hands her a certificate and **BOOK VOUCHERS** from the local bookshop.

SCHOOL READING CHALLENGE

This Most Improved Reading Award is presented to:

OLIVIA

Congratulations!

Ella and Olivia are over the moon! They have both won special prizes! And even though the Reading Challenge is officially finished, they still can't wait to do even *more* reading! After all, **BOOK WEEK** is just around the corner!

COLLECT THEM ALL!

If you liked this book, you'll love reading
OLiViA'S Secret Scribbles and ELLA Diaries